Look Out, Washington, D.C.!

YEARLING BOOKS are designed especially to entertain and enlighten young people. Patricia Reilly Giff, consultant to this series, received her bachelor's degree from Marymount College and a master's degree in history from St. John's University. She holds a Professional Diploma in Reading and a Doctorate of Humane Letters from Hofstra University. She was a teacher and reading consultant for many years, and is the author of numerous books for young readers.

A POLK STREET SPECIAL

Look Out, Washington, D.C.!

. . .

Patricia Reilly Giff
Illustrated by Blanche Sims

A YEARLING BOOK

Published by
Bantam Doubleday Dell Books for Young Readers
a division of
Bantam Doubleday Dell Publishing Group, Inc.
1540 Broadway
New York, New York 10036

The trademarks Yearling® and Dell® are registered in the U.S. Patent and
Trademark Office and other countries.

ISBN: 0-440-40934-9

Printed in the United States of America

June 1995

18 17 16

CWO

To Paula Danziger

Chapter 1

"**T**hink hard," Ms. Rooney was saying.

Emily Arrow tapped her pencil against her teeth. She thought as hard as she could.

The class was studying people this month. Famous people.

"Someone you'd like to be," said Ms. Rooney.

"I'd be a president," said Matthew.

"Which one?" someone asked.

"Yes. Which—" Ms. Rooney put her hand over her mouth. "The lunch money. We forgot again."

Emily watched Dawn Bosco grab the bag. This week Dawn was lunch monitor.

Lucky Dawn.

Emily stuck her hand in the air. She waved hard at Dawn . . . so hard her book fell on the floor.

The book was about pioneers, and a girl named Laura. Emily's mother had given it to her.

"Me," everyone was yelling. "Pick me."

Dawn took a long time picking. "Emily," she said at last. "And Jill Simon."

"Hurry, girls," said Ms. Rooney. "I have a surprise. It's the best one of your life."

Emily grabbed up her book.

She raced down the aisle.

She left the book on the windowsill.

Then she followed Dawn and Jill to the cafeteria. "What do you think the surprise is?"

Jill shook her head. Her four braids bounced around. "I don't know."

Dawn pressed her lips together. "I'm not going to say one word. I don't want to spoil the surprise."

Emily gritted her teeth.

Dawn acted as if she knew everything.

She probably didn't know spit.

On the way back, they saw Beast.

He was hanging from the sink.

"I'm Swinging Sam," he yelled. "The Number One man."

"You're going to pull that sink off the wall," Dawn said.

Mrs. Clark poked her head out of her classroom door. "What are the four of you doing?"

"I'm doing nothing," Dawn said.

"That's the whole trouble." Mrs. Clark frowned at Beast. "You think you're a comedy."

Everyone raced back to the classroom.

Emily wondered what a comedy was.

Ms. Rooney was waiting. "Remember the money we saved?"

Emily remembered. The class had worked on a garage sale. They had washed cars too.

"Here's the news," Ms. Rooney said. "In a few weeks we're going to visit Washington."

"Isn't he a president?" Beast asked.

"Our first president," said Timothy Barbiero.

"I thought he was dead," Matthew said.

Ms. Rooney closed her eyes. "George Washington has been dead for almost two hundred years. We're going to *Washington*,

D.C. It's the city that's named for him, our nation's capital."

"The Number One city," said Timothy.

"I knew it," said Dawn. "I guessed this would be the surprise."

"You're a great guesser," said Beast.

"She's a comedy," said Emily.

Ms. Rooney began again. "We'll take a train. And then—"

The door opened. It was Emily's little sister, Stacy. "May I talk with Emily, please?"

Ms. Rooney nodded. She kept talking. "We'll stay overnight in a bed-and-breakfast. We'll . . ."

Emily couldn't hear the rest. Stacy was whispering in her ear.

"I can't find my picture," Stacy said. "The best one I ever drew. Me with my teeth. I want to show it to my class."

Everyone was clapping now.

"It's with your stuff," Stacy said. "I remember I put it there."

Ms. Rooney was saying something about a diary.

"Take out your books," Stacy whispered. "We'll wiggle them back and forth."

"We'll see the Lincoln Memorial," said Ms. Rooney. "We'll write about that too."

"Em-i-ly," Stacy said.

Emily slammed her books on her desk.

"We'll take them to the White House," Ms. Rooney said.

Stacy was turning pages with a slip-slap noise.

"Take what to the White House?" Emily asked.

No one answered.

Emily flipped through her notebook.

The picture wasn't there.

Stacy stuck out her lip.

She stamped down the aisle and out the door.

Emily looked up.

She had just missed the rest of what Ms. Rooney was saying.

Chapter 2

Emily was counting. Two more days until Washington, D.C.

Right now she was sitting in the backseat of the car.

She was trying to read her Laura book.

Laura was riding in a covered wagon. She was going to live in a house on the prairie.

Emily couldn't read, though.

It was too noisy.

Her baby sister, Caitie, was banging a rattle.

Stacy was singing at the top of her lungs. "Going to Mitch . . . Mitch . . . Mitchell's . . . Department Store."

Her mother looked back through the rearview mirror.

She smiled at Emily. "Give Caitie a pat."

Emily touched the baby's cheek.

Caitie smiled up at her . . . a big smile, without teeth.

Stacy stopped singing. "How come you want to go to Washington, C.D., Emily?"

"D.C.," Emily said. "District of Columbia."

"I hope you don't get lost," Stacy said. "You might never come home again."

Emily shivered. "I hope not too."

"You'll probably be homesick." Stacy

was nodding. "You'll be crying for me all over the place."

Stacy had chocolate pudding around her mouth.

She had chopped her bangs off with scissors.

"I don't think so," said Emily.

Her mother laughed. "You might be just a tiny bit homesick . . . but you're going to learn a lot."

"That reminds me," Emily said. "I have to pick an important person."

"Pick me," said Stacy.

"It has to be someone famous," Emily said. "Someone who did something important for our country."

She sighed. Jill had picked Betsy Ross.

Betsy had made the first American flag.

Too bad Emily hadn't thought of her first.

Emily shook her head. She didn't like to sew anyway.

Emily thought of something else. "If only I could have pajamas with lace. Piles of lace."

"I bet Dawn Bosco has lace," said Stacy. "That's why."

"It is not," said Emily. But it was almost true.

Dawn had said she had the best pajamas in the world. Surprise pajamas.

Inside the store, they took the escalator. "One thing you need," said her mother. "Underwear."

Jill was in the underwear department with her mother.

Mrs. Simon was holding up tan underpants with legs.

"Not like those," Emily whispered.

"Jill catches cold a lot," said Mrs. Simon. "I hope she doesn't catch cold in Washington."

Jill sneezed. Her braids bounced.

"Uh-oh," said Mrs. Simon.

Emily waved at Jill and moved away.

At the next counter, she found pink underwear. It had lace and bows.

"Please?" Emily asked her mother. "Please?"

She would put them on top of her suitcase.

Let Dawn Bosco have a look at those babies.

"You should have tan ones," said Stacy, "with long skinny legs."

"I should not," Emily said.

"You lost my best picture," Stacy said. "Remember?"

Emily shook her head hard.

She could see her mother looking at pajamas.

They had hearts. Red fur hearts.

Emily could hardly breathe. "Number One pajamas."

Her mother smiled. "Well . . ."

Stacy leaned against the counter. "Are we staying here forever?"

"All right," said Mrs. Arrow. "We'll take them."

The line at the counter was long.

Emily watched the lady ring up Jill's tan underwear.

Then at last it was their turn.

Stacy's head was down on the counter. "I saw Dawn Bosco when we came in downstairs," she said. "Buying a purse."

A purse!

"I need one too," Emily said. "A Number One purse."

"I'm sick of Emily being Number One every two minutes," Stacy said.

Her mother frowned. "That's a lot of money."

"I'll give you my fifty cents from Aunt

Eileen," Emily said. "And my quarter from cleaning the garage."

"I guess . . ." Her mother put the package into the bottom of Caitie's stroller.

Downstairs, Emily slung purses over her shoulder.

She could see Jill at the next counter.

Jill was holding up a fat notebook.

Emily couldn't make up her mind.

One purse had red stripes.

The shiny black one had a tiny pad and pencil inside.

Stacy lay on the floor. Her eyes were closed.

Emily could see Derrick Grace in the next department. He had a camera up to his eyes.

The strap was twisted around his neck.

She wondered how he could breathe . . . or see.

It was a good thing he didn't see her.

His mother was holding up a pair of boys' underpants.

Emily looked back at Jill.

Something was tugging at the back of her mind. It had to do with a notebook. Something Ms. Rooney had said.

She couldn't remember what it was.

Emily took the shiny black purse.

Too bad she wouldn't have money to put inside.

Not one cent.

Chapter 3

At last it was time to leave. The train station was long and almost dark. Emily was sleepy.

She had never gotten up so early in her whole life.

"Stay together," Ms. Rooney called.

"Don't worry." Jill Simon yanked at her suitcase. "I'm sticking to you like glue."

Emily tried to stick like glue too.

Her suitcase was heavy. It dragged along the walk.

Good thing her mother had told her to leave out her checkers game and three extra shirts.

"You won't have time for all this anyway," her mother had said.

And Stacy had told her, "Too bad you don't have time to find my picture."

"I—DO—NOT—HAVE—YOUR—PICTURE." Emily said each word as loudly as she could.

Stacy gave the suitcase a kick.

Emily made a fish face. She pushed her suitcase toward the door.

Then she turned back to say goodbye.

Stacy was kneeling in front of the closet. She was throwing everything out.

Too bad for Stacy.

Oof. Emily bumped into someone.

"Careful," someone said. It was Mr. O'Brien, Wayne's grandfather. He had come on the trip to help Ms. Rooney.

Timothy Barbiero's mother had come too. Right now she was yelling.

"My nerves," she kept saying.

The boys were playing Got You Last.

Mrs. Barbiero's face was red. She was trying to run after them.

Derrick Grace was one inch away from the end of the platform.

He was taking a picture of the tracks.

Ms. Rooney turned around. "Some people might end up going home."

Quickly everyone caught up with the line.

"We have to pick partners," Ms. Rooney said.

But just then Emily heard a long *hoot-hoot*. The wind roared through the tunnel.

The train whooshed into the station.

"Never mind partners yet," said Ms. Rooney. She pointed. "Hurry."

"Something went in my eye," Jill said. "I can feel it."

Emily bumped her suitcase along the platform.

She got farther and farther behind.

Even Derrick Grace was ahead of her . . . and he had stopped to take a picture of the sign on the wall: PENNSYLVANIA STATION.

Emily was puffing by the time she followed the class inside the train.

"Pillows on the chairs," yelled Beast. "Number One."

Emily raced for a window seat.

She landed on top of Dawn Bosco.

"Too late," Dawn said. "You're a comedy."

All the window seats were taken.

Maybe she'd sit on the aisle next to Jill.

But Jill was crying . . . making a lot of noise. "I still have something in my eye. Something huge."

Too bad for Jill.

Emily sank down next to Dawn.

Dawn had taken up most of the room.

Three purses.

Two sweaters over her arm. One had pearls on the sleeves. The other had diamonds.

Emily scrunched into the skinny space. She tried to shove Dawn over with her elbow.

Dawn didn't budge.

Forget Dawn for a partner. Maybe she'd pick Linda Lorca, or Sherri Dent.

The train began to move.

Emily looked out the window. It seemed as if the station were moving, not the train.

For a moment she wished the train weren't moving. She wished she could race home. Her mother and father would be in the kitchen. Caitie would be in her high chair. And Stacy . . .

"It was hard to pack, wasn't it?" Dawn said.

"Yes, really," Emily said. "I had to leave a pile of shirts home."

"Me too," said Dawn. "Seven."

Emily crossed her fingers. "Eight."

Dawn said something under her breath.

It sounded like "Forget you for a partner."

The train was out of the station now. They were in the light. Gray buildings rushed by.

"One thing I didn't forget." Dawn held up a fat red notebook.

A diary. Now Emily remembered. She had seen Jill buying a fat notebook in Mitchell's Department Store.

Dawn opened her diary. "I'm going to dedicate this right now."

"Ded-i-cate?" Emily had heard that word somewhere.

"You know . . . put a person's name in front. Just the way they do in books."

"Of course," Emily said.

"I think I'll dedicate it to my important person, Sally Ride."

Emily tried to remember who Sally was.

She could see Derrick on the floor. He was taking a picture of Beast sitting on a pillow.

"The first woman in space," said Dawn.

"Of course," said Emily again.

She pulled out her Laura book. She wasn't even going to talk to Dawn.

The book was stuffed with old homework pages. She was using them for a bookmark.

Right now she was at the part where the Ingalls family had crossed into Kansas.

They were eating cornbread in the wagon.

Dawn gave her a little shove. "My diary is going to be the greatest."

"The greatest what?"

"The greatest diary of Washington, D.C.," said Dawn. "Don't you have one?"

Emily crossed her fingers again. She nodded.

"Good thing," said Dawn. "Remember we have to write everything down that we see. Ms. Rooney is bringing the diaries straight to the president."

Emily looked out the window again. This was going to be some trip.

She didn't have a person to dedicate her diary to.

She didn't even have a diary.

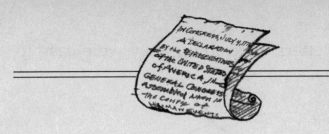

Chapter 4

It seemed as if they had been on the train forever. Emily was sick of looking at telephone poles and backyards.

She peeked over at Dawn.

Dawn had written about a hundred things in her diary already . . . and they weren't even there yet.

Across the aisle, Timothy Barbiero was writing too.

His letters were so big they were easy to see.

The Capitol building is old. It is round on top. It is where the people make the laws.

Timothy was the smartest kid in the class.

Too bad. His diary would never be Number One.

Timothy was a terrible artist.

Besides, the president probably knew all that stuff about the Capitol Building already.

She felt a lump of worry.

What would Ms. Rooney say when she found out Emily didn't have a diary?

Then suddenly she remembered. There was a pad in her new purse.

So what if it was a skinny-minny pad?

A diary was a diary.

She snapped open the purse and pulled it out.

Dawn raised one eyebrow. "That's your diary?"

Emily thought about reaching over. She'd grab Dawn's nose. She'd give it a tweak.

She could almost hear Dawn honking.

Emily almost laughed thinking about it.

She turned so that Dawn couldn't see her writing.

She left a line for her dedication. Then in her best teeny-tiny writing, she wrote:

I am on the train.
I am going to Washington.

She slapped the pad shut.

Dawn was covering most of her writing. But Emily could see a little of it anyway.

I have a brand-new coat for the trip.

Emily watched a few more telephone poles.

Maybe she should write that she was wearing a beautiful coat. No. If the president saw her, he'd know it was a lie.

She was wearing her old blue jacket. Her mother had sewn up a rip in the pocket yesterday.

Besides, she didn't have that much room in her diary.

After all, it had only a couple of tiny pages.

She had to save it for Washington, D.C.

At last the train pulled to a stop. "Union Station," the conductor yelled.

"I thought we were going to Washington," said Beast.

Beast was right. Emily nodded at Ms. Rooney.

Let Ms. Rooney see she was paying attention.

But Ms. Rooney shook her head. "Union Station *is* in Washington."

Emily stopped nodding. She hoped no one had seen.

Ms. Rooney was still talking about the

railroad station. "Union Station was built before I was born," she said. "It looks like a palace. It has about a hundred stores . . . and a bunch of movie—"

Whoompf. Something landed on top of Emily.

It was Derrick Grace with his camera. "Watch out, Emily," he said. "I've got only one chance to take this picture."

Now he was leaning across Dawn.

"You think you're a comedy," Dawn told him.

Ms. Rooney looked at her watch. "We'll have to hurry. A bus is waiting."

Emily stood up quickly. She wanted to see Union Station looking like a palace. And she wanted a window seat in the bus.

"Not so fast," Ms. Rooney said.

Emily sank back in her seat.

"We have to have partners," said Ms.

Rooney. "We have to watch out for each other."

Emily sniffed. Dawn wasn't even looking at her.

Maybe Jill.

But Jill and Linda were standing in the aisle. They were pointing at each other.

In two seconds everyone had a partner.

Everyone but Emily.

And Derrick Grace.

Derrick was standing on Jill's armrest.

He was pointing his camera at the window.

"All right," said Ms. Rooney. "Everybody set?"

Emily began to shake her head, no.

Ms. Rooney looked around. "Derrick. Derrick and Emily. Nice choice."

Emily looked at Derrick out of the corner of her eye.

Horrible choice.

It looked as if Derrick thought so too.
They were the last two off the train.
The last two on the bus.

Derrick slid into the window seat before she could beat him to it.

Then she remembered. She hadn't even taken time to look at Union Station.

Chapter 5

The bus driver rode up and down streets. He looped around traffic circles.

Derrick took up most of the room in front of the window.

He was snapping pictures a mile a minute.

Emily gritted her teeth. "I'd like to see," she said.

He turned to look at her.

Emily tried to smile. Her mother always said, "Be nice to everyone."

Derrick snapped her picture. "Great smile," he said.

Emily blinked. "Thanks."

"Can't give you much room," he said. "Trying to get Number One pictures. Going to get them straight to the president."

"But . . . ," Emily began.

"He's going to love them," said Derrick.

Emily tried to sit up as tall as she could. She looked out a little piece of window on top.

She had never seen so many buildings in her life.

The bus slowed down at one with a round top.

"I think that's the Lincoln Memorial," said Dawn.

"Not yet," said Timothy.

Emily stared at the white building. Then she remembered. Round top. "Hey, it's the Capitol."

"Yes," said Timothy.

"Wonderful," said Ms. Rooney.

The bus started up again. A moment later it stopped at a tall skinny building.

On top were two red lights.

"Just like eyes," Emily said.

Dawn pointed. "It's the Lincoln Memorial."

Emily watched Timothy. He was shaking his head, no. "It's the Washington Monument," he said. "Eight hundred ninety-seven steps to the top."

The bus door opened. "We don't have to walk up," said Ms. Rooney. "We'll take an elevator."

They waited in line for a long time. It made Emily think of Mitchell's Department Store.

It made her think of Stacy.

Stacy hadn't gotten a purse. She hadn't gotten lace underwear . . . and she hadn't even minded.

Flags were whipping in the wind around the Washington Monument.

Emily tried to think about the flags instead of Stacy.

At last the class whooshed to the top in the elevator.

It was crowded up there.

Derrick rested his camera on her shoulder.

Down below, Emily could see all of Washington. Ms. Rooney pointed out the White House, where the president lived.

"The floor is moving," Dawn said. "I can feel it in my feet."

That Dawn. "Don't be silly . . . ," Emily began. Then she felt it too.

"Dawn is right," said Wayne's grandfather. "The building sways a little in the wind."

"My nerves," said Mrs. Barbiero.

"I want to get out of here," Jill said.

Emily wanted to get out of there too. But she saw something below.

Bunches of pink. Here and there. A beautiful soft—

She knew what it was even before Ms. Rooney told them.

"Cherry blossoms," said Ms. Rooney. "Long ago the Japanese people gave us three thousand cherry trees."

Emily remembered. Her mother had planted a cherry tree in their yard. She had told Emily about the cherry trees in Washington.

If only her mother were here now.

Emily thought of her mother all the way down in the elevator.

She thought of her as the bus started up again . . .

Emily swallowed.

She hadn't said goodbye to Stacy.

She remembered kissing Caitie.

Caitie had been sitting in her jump seat.

She had been crying and waving her arms.

Then Emily's mother had beeped the car horn.

Emily closed her eyes.

When she opened them, Derrick was pointing the camera at her.

Emily smiled quickly.

"I already took your picture," he said. "I have to save some film."

Emily stopped smiling. She watched as the bus moved slowly along the road.

"There's the Lincoln Memorial," said Timothy.

"I thought so," said Dawn. "He's the one on the penny."

Emily sat up straight. She had a terrific idea.

President Lincoln could be her important person.

She opened her mouth.

"I'm picking him," said Beast. "I'd like to be on a penny too."

Emily closed her mouth again. She looked out the window at the Lincoln Memorial.

There was a huge white statue of President Lincoln.

He looked tired. He looked a little sad.

Emily was beginning to feel sad too.

She wished she had kissed everyone goodbye.

She wouldn't see them for two whole days.

Next to her Derrick was talking to himself. He was saying something about taking a picture of a moon rock.

Emily looked across the aisle. Jill and Linda were talking together.

Dawn was writing in her diary.

Emily thought about writing in her diary too.

She could say that there were fifty-six steps up to the statue of Lincoln. One for every year he had lived.

She could say there was a secret cave underneath the statue.

Her mother had told her all that.

She didn't, though.

There just wasn't enough room in the diary.

Chapter 6

"**N**ext stop, Rock Creek Park," said Ms. Rooney. "And the National Zoo."

Timothy began to read his diary aloud.

"A giant panda is at the zoo. He was given to us by the Chinese people. There's a rhinoceros too, and apes . . ."

"That's you," Matthew told Beast. "An ape."

"I'm a boa constrictor." Beast jumped on Matthew's back.

"I'm at my wits' end," said Mrs. Barbiero.

Wayne's grandfather laughed.

The bus door opened.

"Meet here," said Ms. Rooney. "Don't get lost. Don't talk to strangers."

Before Emily could move, Derrick hopped over her.

Emily was last out again.

She marched along in back of Jill and Linda.

Up in front, Ms. Rooney was calling, "Stay with your partners."

Derrick didn't stop moving.

He snapped a picture of a dead tree.

Then he snapped one of Matthew on a pile of rocks.

Emily was out of breath chasing after him.

In the cafeteria he was still one step ahead of her.

That Derrick.

In school he never said a word.

Emily followed him across the cafeteria.

He wasn't good at math or reading.

He wasn't bad either.

She tried to think.

He really wasn't good or bad at anything.

Derrick was just a blob.

And right now, the blob was kneeling up on the cafeteria rail.

He was taking a picture of the knives, and forks, and trays.

Emily put her hands on her hips. "We have to sit together, you know. Ms. Rooney said that partners have to . . ."

Derrick slid onto a bench.

Emily sat down across from him.

Everyone else was halfway across the room.

"How about we move . . . ," Emily began.

"Hurry up and eat," he said. "I've got to take more pictures . . . as fast as I can."

"Where's your lunch?" Emily asked.

"I left it somewhere." He raised his shoulders in the air. "On the train . . . or the bus . . ."

"You're going to starve." Emily opened her lunch.

She wondered what her mother had made.

Egg salad. She could smell it.

Derrick was sitting there . . . doing nothing.

"Why . . . ," she began.

He sighed. "You're my partner. I have to wait for you."

Emily opened her eyes. Derrick had a nice face when you took a good look at him. "How about some of my sandwich?" she asked.

"Well . . ."

"It's egg salad. Crunchy, with celery." She pulled out half her sandwich.

She slid the Baggie with the other half toward him.

He finished it in two bites.

He ate two of her cookies, half her soda, and all of her apple.

"Whew," she said. "I haven't even finished my part of the sandwich."

She took the last bite and stood up.

Derrick crumpled the bag. He scooped up Emily's crusts.

He threw everything in the litter basket.

Emily looked back at Dawn's table.

Dawn was talking with Linda.

Jill was talking with Beast.

Everyone was having a good time.

She saw Timothy pointing.

They were pointing at Derrick.

Derrick was standing on tiptoe.

He was bent over the litter basket.

Emily couldn't see his head.

He threw out a bunch of stuff.

A couple of milk containers. A brown paper bag.

When he stood up, he was holding something.

He threw everything else back in. Then he called to Emily, "Let's go. I want to take a picture of the panda."

Emily looked back at the table. Everyone was fooling around.

Emily sighed.

Derrick couldn't go without her.

"All right," she said.

They raced out the door.

He stopped ahead of her. "I saw this at the last minute."

He had something in his hand.

It was Emily's Baggie from lunch.

"There's a note inside," he was saying. "It must have been in with your sandwich."

Emily could see it now too.

> I LOVE YOU, EMILY.
>   XXX MOM

Emily took a breath.

Derrick was grinning. "I knew that would make you feel better."

Before she could say anything, Derrick was disappearing around the corner.

"Hey, wait up," she yelled.

She ran to catch up with him.

Chapter 7

They were on the bus again.
Emily pulled out her diary.
In skinny-minny handwriting she wrote:

We saw Smokey the Bear
at the zoo.
Derrick took his picture.

Ms. Rooney stood up. She held on to the rail. "We're coming to a special part of the trip now. The National Air and Space Museum."

Timothy opened his diary. "I wrote about it already," he said. "It's the museum about flying, and missiles, and . . ."

He raised his shoulders in the air. "It's all about the air around us . . . the space . . . out as far as—"

"—the planets and even farther than that," said Dawn in a rush. "Are we going to sit here forever?"

The bus doors opened.

Derrick turned to Emily. "This is where I'll get my best picture. It's the moon rock."

"What's a moon rock?" Emily asked.

Derrick pointed. "Look up. What do you see?"

"The sky," Emily said. "A tiny cloud—"

"The moon," said Derrick. "Look at it."

"I am," Emily said. She remembered her mother showing her the daytime moon when she was in kindergarten.

She remembered her mother holding her up, saying, "See, Emily, it doesn't go away."

"Emily?" Derrick asked. "Are you listening?"

She nodded. "It's big and round and—"

"Missing a rock," said Derrick. "A piece of rock from the moon is right inside the museum. We can even touch it."

"The moon isn't round like a plate," she remembered her mother telling her. *"It's round like an orange."*

It had been hard to believe that in kindergarten.

And now, staring up at the moon, she could see dark spots.

"Mountains," said Derrick. "Deep holes . . ."

Dawn came up behind them.

"Look at the moon," Emily told her.

Dawn pushed her hair back. She was wearing tiny moon earrings. "Out of my way, guys. I'm on my way to see *Skylab*. I'll probably live in space someday."

Emily made a fish face as Dawn pushed past.

Then she looked up at the moon again. She walked backward into the museum.

Maybe her mother was outside at home, she thought.

Maybe she was looking at the moon too.

"Look where you're going," Derrick said. "You're going to fall—"

Too late.

Emily slid across the floor.

She tried to catch herself, but there was nothing to hold on to.

Oof. She went down hard.

She could see the ceiling way above her.

It was so high, it might almost be the sky.

Planes were hanging from the top.

Emily could feel her elbow stinging.

She knew it was bleeding.

"Look at Emily!" Jill yelled. "I can't stand blood."

Emily stood up slowly.

She could see Timothy pointing to one of the planes on the ceiling.

It wasn't much bigger than a car.

"There's my person," said Timothy. "Charles Lindbergh."

"There's a guy up there?" Beast was asking.

Emily's other elbow was stinging too.

She bit her lip. She didn't want to cry in front of everyone.

"Of course not," Timothy said. "That's his plane, *The Spirit of St. Louis*. He flew that little plane all the way across the ocean. He was the first one."

Everyone was so lucky, Emily thought. Everyone had found a person. If she could just . . .

If she could just find a handkerchief.

If she could just not cry.

If she could just see her mother for two minutes.

And her father.

And Stacy and Caitie.

Everyone else was racing across the room.

Everyone except Derrick.

"I think you need a Band-Aid," he said.

She nodded.

That Derrick was turning out to be a great kid.

Ms. Rooney came over to them. "On the bus," she told Emily. "In a big green bag on the front seat. I have a pile of bandages."

Emily nodded.

"You need someone to go with you," said Ms. Rooney.

"Don't worry," Derrick said. "I'll go."

"I'll go too," said Wayne's grandfather.

They went back out the door. There were a million buses all over the place.

It took a long time to find theirs.

At last they climbed up the steps.

They said a quick hello to the bus driver.

They turned Ms. Rooney's bag upside down.

Band-Aids flew out. So did a book, an apple, a pair of sunglasses.

Emily pulled up her sleeves.

She slapped on the Band-Aids.

She made a fish face just for fun.

Derrick snapped a picture of her with Wayne's grandfather.

Then they dashed back to the museum.

They looked at another bunch of old planes.

They looked at satellites.

"I'm saving the moon rock for last," Derrick said.

They stopped in front of one of the spacecraft. "It's *Gemini 4*," Derrick said.

Gemini 4 was tiny, Emily thought. She wouldn't want to sit inside it for a long time.

"They took the first space walk from *Gemini*," said Derrick.

He turned the corner ahead of her.

They passed Dawn. She was writing in her diary as fast as she could.

Derrick stopped again. "See that picture on the wall?"

Emily nodded. It was a man in a space suit. "Is he standing on the moon?"

Derrick nodded. "It's Neil Armstrong in 1969. He was the first man on the moon."

Emily looked at Derrick. She was surprised he knew all that stuff.

He was turning out to be a really great kid.

In front of them was a rock.

Emily reached out and touched it.

"It feels like an ordinary rock," she said. "A big plain old—"

"Very old," said Derrick. "Four billion years old."

He pulled off his jacket. "This is what I've been waiting for.

"Isn't this going to be the best picture?" he asked. "Better than a diary—"

He broke off. "My important person is a man who takes pictures. His name is Edward Steichen. Sometime I'll show you . . ."

He pushed the camera button.

Nothing happened.

He pushed again.

Emily leaned forward.

"I'm out of film." He looked as if he wanted to cry.

"Maybe we could buy . . ."

"I don't have any money," he said.

Emily raised her shoulders in the air. "I don't either, or—"

But before she could finish, she heard Mrs. Barbiero calling.

"You're the last two. Everyone else is on the bus. Hurry. It's going to leave without us."

There wasn't another minute to think about what to do.

They just had to follow Mrs. Barbiero back to the bus.

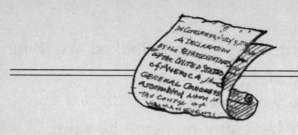

Chapter 8

Emily couldn't stop yawning.

The class had stopped for hamburgers at McDonald's.

Even Beast and Matthew were tired.

They hadn't run around once.

And Derrick hadn't said a word since they had left the museum.

Now they were in the bed-and-breakfast.

It was a big house . . . big enough for the whole class.

Ms. Rooney stood at the end of the hall.

"Boys in the end room," she said. "With Mr. O'Brien."

Emily thought about her room at home. She thought about Stacy in the next bed. She wished she were with Stacy right now.

"In the middle room . . ." Ms. Rooney pointed to Linda. "You, Sherri, and . . ."

"Me," said Dawn.

"And me too," said Ms. Rooney. "Jill and Emily in the corner room with Mrs. Barbiero."

Emily and Jill went into the room together.

It was pink. The bedspreads had yellow roses. "Beautiful," said Emily. She couldn't wait to tell her mother.

"I've been thinking about my own room," said Jill. "And my mother."

Emily nodded.

Mrs. Barbiero smiled. "Don't worry. I'll be right here."

She sank down on the rocking chair. "I just have to close my eyes for two minutes."

From the window Emily watched the red lights on the Washington Monument.

She sat down on her bed. Jill was tugging her suitcase open.

Emily thought about opening hers too.

The Number One lace-and-ribbons underwear was on top.

Poor Jill with her long tan underpants.

Emily knelt on the floor. She opened her suitcase a tiny bit.

She shoved the underwear to the bottom.

There was a knock on the door.

It was Dawn . . . in a nightgown with fur hearts.

"Same as mine," said Emily.

"Same as mine too." Jill laughed. "Except mine is a little bigger."

Footsteps exploded down the hall.

Beast was chasing Matthew.

Beast had on red ski-pants pajama bottoms. He had on a blue top.

His undershirt dribbled out from underneath.

Everyone was in the hall now. They raced back and forth.

"My nerves," said Mrs. Barbiero.

A woman poked her head out a door. "What are you kids doing?"

"We're a comedy," said Dawn, dashing past.

The woman laughed. She closed her door again.

Ms. Rooney came out. She was wearing purple sweats.

Emily sounded out the word on the front: "Dar-ling."

"This was a long day," Ms. Rooney said.

Everyone raced for the rooms.

"Good-night, Darling," Beast called.

Emily was the last one back in her room.

Mrs. Barbiero was still in the rocker. She was sound asleep.

She didn't even hear Jill bouncing on the bed.

"I—have—to—work—on—my—diary," said Jill with each bounce.

"Me too," said Emily.

What could she pick to say? What would fit in the skinny space that was left?

Jill stopped bouncing. "I'd like to have the Number One diary," she said. "I'd like to be the Number One person. Just once."

Emily felt surprised. She thought she was

the only one who wanted to be Number One.

And Dawn.

And maybe the president.

Emily went through her suitcase and her purse.

Where was her toothbrush?

She dumped everything out on the floor. Socks, a sweater, her book.

"Papers just flew out of your book," Jill said.

Emily reached for them. "Old homework."

Jill laughed. "Here's a picture of a monster too."

Emily closed her eyes.

She knew what it was before she looked.

It was the Stacy-with-her-teeth picture.

It had been in the book all this time.

Poor Stacy. Maybe she had wanted to be

Number One too . . . showing everyone her picture.

"What's the matter?" Jill asked.

Emily shook her head. She couldn't talk.

Jill slid off the bed. "Emily?"

"I miss my sister . . . ," Emily began and stopped.

Jill patted her shoulder.

She helped Emily put her things back into the suitcase.

Jill picked up a ball of socks. "These are really heavy."

She tossed the socks into the suitcase.

They landed with a clunk.

"Something's inside." Emily reached over. She unrolled them.

A lump of paper was inside.

It had a crooked number 1 written on it.

Coins were folded inside.

"It's Stacy's money from Aunt Eileen,"

Emily said slowly. "She knew I didn't have any for a souvenir."

Jill went back to her bed. "I wish I had a sister."

Emily climbed into her own bed.

By tomorrow night she'd be home.

She could feel herself falling asleep.

Everything was mixed up in her mind. A big number 1. Dawn. And Derrick. And the Washington Monument with its two red eyes.

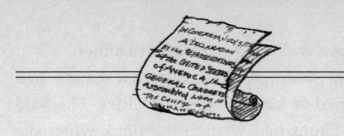

Chapter 9

In the hall Ms. Rooney was clapping her hands. "Don't forget anything."

Emily took one last look at the room.

"Oops," she said. "My book."

Mrs. Barbiero handed it to her. "I loved this book too," she said. "Laura was a wonderful person, a pioneer."

Emily nodded. "She went across the country in a covered wagon."

They walked downstairs together.

Mrs. Barbiero told her that Laura had married a farmer named Wilder. She said that Laura had written the book when she was old.

In the dining room Emily chose pancakes.

Almost everyone else had chosen pancakes too.

Dawn was on Emily's other side eating. She was writing in her diary too.

Emily saw a drop of pancake syrup on the page.

Dawn saw it too. She drew a circle around the spot.

THIS IS WHAT WE ATE FOR BREKFEST, she wrote.

They looked at each other.

Emily started to laugh.

Dawn laughed too.

It looked as if they were friends again.

They ate fast.

The souvenir shop was next door.

Everyone scrambled inside.

"I'm getting a Number One present for myself," Beast yelled. "Something for twenty cents."

"What you're going to get," said the counter lady, "is put out of here. Calm down."

Emily walked around the store slowly.

She needed two things.

The first one was easy.

She found the second one a moment later.

Perfect.

Just before she left, she stopped.

She saw a pile of books.

Book about presidents, and Washington, D.C., and even the covered wagons going west.

Emily reached out to touch one.

It gave her the most wonderful idea.

She stood there another minute.

Then she followed Derrick back onto the bus.

"I hope your diaries are ready," said Ms. Rooney.

Emily pulled hers out.

She was glad her pencil had an eraser.

By the time they pulled up to the White House, she had erased what she had written.

"Look," said Ms. Rooney.

Ahead was the most beautiful house Emily had ever seen.

"It's not just the president's house," said Ms. Rooney. "It belongs to all of us."

Emily stared at the White House windows.

Maybe the president was behind one of them.

"Any one of you could be president someday," said Ms. Rooney.

Emily smoothed out her paper.

She had two minutes to write her whole diary.

First the dedication to her important person.

She wrote it as tiny as she could.

TO LAURA INGALLS WILDER

A NUMBER 1 PIONEER

Then, underneath, she began:

Dear Mr. President,

I loved Washington. D.C. It has many things like soovenear shops.

I found out something. Everyone wants to be Number 1. The nicest peple let other peple be Number 1 sometimes.

Like Jill. Like Derrick. Like Stacy.

Emily closed her diary.

She patted her souvenir bag.

Inside were two postcards. One showed the moon rock.

That was for Derrick.

The other showed a girl in front of the White House.

She looked just like Stacy.

Stacy could bring it to school with her teeth picture.

Emily hopped off the bus.

She couldn't wait to see the Red Room, and the Blue Room, and . . . she couldn't remember if they had any other colors.

In front of her, Ms. Rooney was taking diaries. "The president will love them."

Emily hoped so.

"Number One," Beast was yelling.

Emily yelled it too.

Then she straightend her shoulders.

She marched up the path to the White House.

The Polk Street
Guide to
Washington, D.C.

The Polk Street Kids' Favorite Places to Visit in Washington, D.C. (listed in alphabetical order)

```
HOMEWORK:
Pick your favorite place
in Washington, D.C. Tell us
about it.  At least 25
words, please.
```

Ms. Rooney pointed to the chalk-board. "Don't forget to copy your homework," she said.

Beast pulled out his assignment pad. "I hate homework."

"Do you think I love it?" asked Matthew.

"All that writing stuff," said Jill. "My fingers get tired."

Ms. Rooney laughed. "This is the easiest homework in the world."

Dawn raised her hand. "We can write about any place in Washington? Like shopping and—"

"—flying kites." Emily looked out the window. "You can fly your kite in front of the Washington Monument on a windy day. *Whoosh* . . ."

"How about the egg-rolling contest?" Dawn said. "It's at the White House, the day after Easter. You can see a giant Easter bunny . . ."

"And there's a decorated egg contest," said someone else.

"And—" Emily began.

Mr. Mancina popped his head into the room. He looked at the chalkboard. "I'd write about Mount Vernon. It's only a bus ride away from Washington. It's the farm where George Washington lived."

Ms. Rooney nodded. "And what about the places we saw on our trip? We could put them all in a book."

"Yes," said Dawn Bosco. "I'm going to put my name on top in big letters . . ."

THE WHITE HOUSE

The White House by Dawn Tiffany Bosco:

My favorite place? Easy. The *White House*. That's the place where the presidents live . . . all except

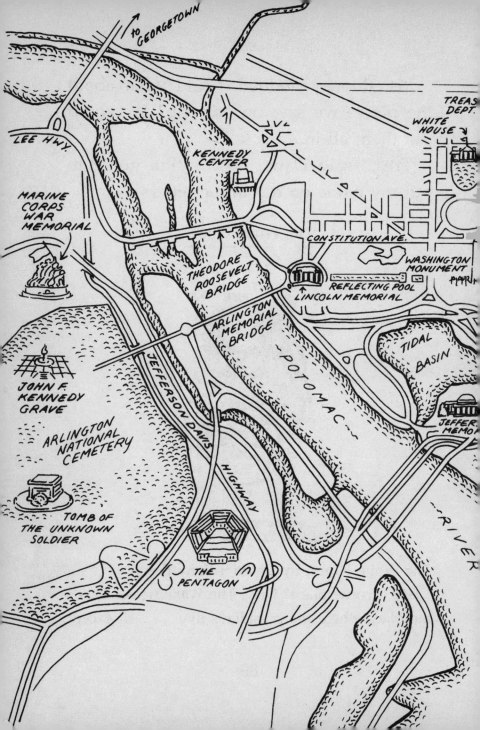

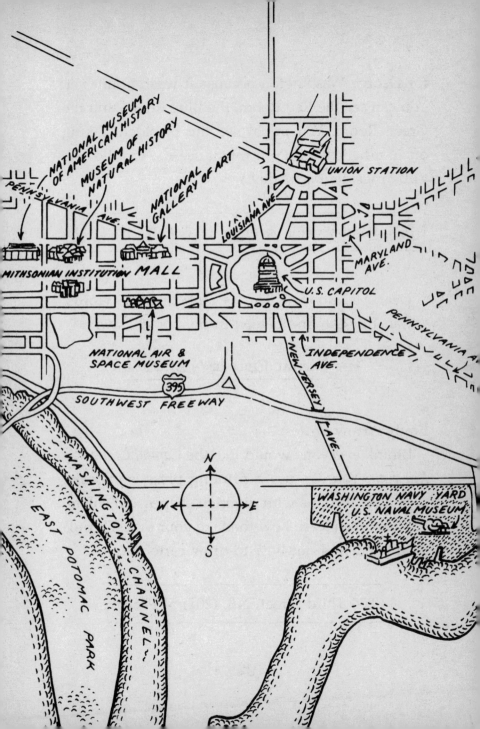

for George Washington because it wasn't built yet. You can see the Red Room, the Blue Room, and the Green Room. You might see the president taking off in a helicopter. (You might see me too. I'd like to be president someday.)

1600 Pennsylvania Avenue, NW, (202) 456-7041

Dear Ms. Rooney: This is more than 25 words. Can I be the first person in the book? Dawn

THE CAPITAL CHILDREN'S MUSEUM

Emily Arrow writes:

I think everyone would like the *Capital Children's Museum*. You can use a printing press, and make computer pictures with different shapes and colors. You can even learn how to make your own TV program, and find out how to draw cartoons.

800 Third Street, NE, (202) 543-8600

Jason Basyk says:

Take an *FBI* tour. (*Federal Bureau of Investigation.*) You'll see how criminals are caught. You can watch an agent shooting targets in the indoor range. Don't miss the mini spy cameras, and the walking stick that becomes a shotgun.

J. Edgar Hoover Building, E Street between Ninth and Tenth streets, NW, (202) 324-3447

FORD'S THEATER AND THE PETERSEN HOUSE

A note from Ms. Rooney:

Just up the street from the FBI is *Ford's Theater*. President Lincoln was shot here. He was taken across the street to the *Petersen House*. He died there the next morning. It's a sad place to see.

Ford's Theater, 511 Tenth Street, NW, (202) 426-6924

Petersen House, 516 Tenth Street, NW, (202) 426-6830

THE WASHINGTON DOLLS' HOUSE AND TOY MUSEUM

Jill Simon says:

Don't miss the *Washington Dolls' House and Toy Museum*. You'll see dolls, and toys, and a tiny Capitol Building, and Noah's Ark. There's even a little hat store and a circus tent with clowns.

5236 Forty-fourth Street, NW, (202) 244-0024

THE DAUGHTERS OF THE
AMERICAN REVOLUTION MUSEUM

A note from Ms. Rooney:

If you like dolls and toys that are more than a hundred years old, visit the *Daughters of the American Revolution Museum*. You'll see schoolbooks used by pioneer children too. You might take a Colonial Adventure tour. You'll find out how people lived when our country was young.

1776 D Street, NW, (202) 879-3241

THE LIBRARY OF CONGRESS

Mrs. Baker at the library wants you to know:

The *Library of Congress* has more books than any other library in the world. You can take a tour, or watch a film about the library in Room 139 of the Madison Building. You'll also see the Gutenberg Bible. It's over five hundred years old. (And that's older than I am!)

10 First Street (First and East Capitol streets), SE, (202) 707-5458

THE SUPREME COURT

Wayne O'Brien says:

Maybe you'd like the *Supreme Court*. This is the highest court in the country. You can see a film and look at pictures about the court. If the court is in session, and there's room, you could watch for a few minutes. The judges wear black robes and sit in front of a red curtain.

First and East Capitol streets, NE, (202) 479-3000

THE CAPITOL BUILDING

Wayne's grandfather says:

Congress meets at the *Capitol Building* to make the laws. You can tell when Congress is working. Look for the flags over the House and the Senate. A light shines on the Goddess of Freedom statue on top of the Capitol too. Inside you'll walk through the rotunda (a round hall). Look up to see the dome. The ceilings in Statuary Hall are curved so that whispers can be heard from one side of the room to the other. (Aren't you glad the classroom isn't like that?) Outside, rest on the west lawn.

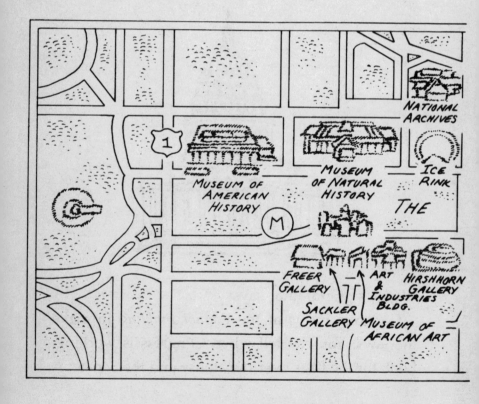

Watch the water splashing in the fountains and over the rocks. Climb up on the Ulysses S. Grant Memorial.

East end of the Mall on Capitol Hill, (202) 225-6827

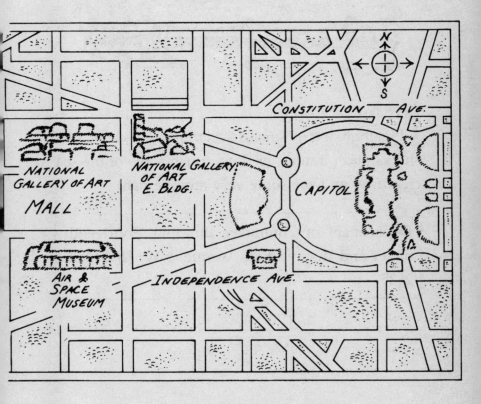

Derrick Grace says:

I really like the *National Aquarium*. You can watch sharks and piranhas feeding, touch some of the sea creatures, and see some very strange fish!

Department of Commerce Building, Fourteenth Street and Constitution Avenue, NW, (202) 482-2825

Noah Green writes:

What about the *Washington Navy Yard*? It opened almost two hundred years ago as a gun factory. Now it's a park. You can climb on old guns and explore the destroyer *John Barry*. You can visit the *U.S. Naval Museum* and try out a submarine periscope. If you like parades, you might see one at the *U.S. Marine Museum*.

Ninth and M streets, SE: Navy Yard and Museum, Building 76, (202) 433-4882; Marine Corps Museum, Building 58, (202) 433-3534

ARLINGTON NATIONAL CEMETERY

Alex Walker says:

See *Arlington National Cemetery* for soldiers, sailors, and marines. Many famous people are also buried there, including President John Kennedy. The Tomb of the Unknown Soldier always has a guard, even all night. He marches twenty-one steps, then faces the tomb for twenty-one seconds. It's like a twenty-one-gun salute.

Arlington, Virginia, (703) 692-0931

ARLINGTON HOUSE (LEE MANSION)

A note from Ms. Rooney:

See *Arlington House* (*Lee Mansion*) at the same time. Don't miss the playroom with old toys.

Arlington, Virginia, (703) 557-0613

THE VIETNAM VETERANS MEMORIAL

Sherri Dent says:

Don't forget the *Vietnam Veterans Memorial*. It's a shiny black stone wall that reflects the sky and the trees. It has the names of more than 58,000 Americans who died in the Vietnam War. People leave pictures, flowers, and medals there.

Constitution Avenue between Henry Bacon Drive and Twenty-first Street, NW, (202) 634-1568

THE WASHINGTON MONUMENT
AND THE REFLECTING POOL

Mrs. Barbiero says:

You can't miss the *Washington Monument*. An elevator will take you to the top. (It's high. My nerves!) You'll see the city down below. The stones that make up the walls come from different cities and states, and some are from as far away as Japan and Turkey. Fireworks on July 4th!

And don't fall in the *Reflecting Pool.* Just watch the ducks in the summer. Bring your ice skates in the winter. The pool is between the Washington Monument and the Lincoln Memorial.

The Mall between Fifteenth and Seventeenth streets, (202) 426-6839

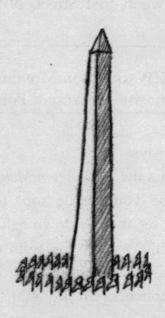

THE LINCOLN MEMORIAL

Linda Lorca writes:

See the *Lincoln Memorial*. There's a huge statue of President Lincoln. He's looking toward the Reflecting Pool and the Washington Monument. I think he looks sad, but very kind. Most people say the monument is most beautiful at night with the lights.

Memorial Circle between Constitution and Independence avenues, (202) 426-6841

Constitution Gardens
and the Jefferson Memorial

Linda Lorca   *****For extra credit*****

You could see *Constitution Gardens.* Most people call this the Duck Pond. It's a park with gardens and a lake. Use the wooden bridge to cross to an island. There are fifty-six benches. Each one is for a person who signed a very important paper. The paper is called the Declaration of Independence. It was signed in the 1700s.

Twenty-third Street and Constitution Avenue, NW, between the Washington Monument and the Lincoln Memorial, (202) 634-1568

*****And for more extra credit*******

Don't miss the *Jefferson Memorial*. This is a huge statue of our third president. Try to see it at night when it is lighted.

South bank of the Tidal Basin at Fourteenth Street and East Basin Drive, SW, East Potomac Park, (202) 426-6841

THE TIDAL BASIN

Richard Best writes:

Check out the paddleboats at the *Tidal Basin*.

Two people fit in a boat. Bring an adult.

It's cool.

Splish splash

splish splash.

Tidal Basin Boathouse, Fifteenth Street and Maine Avenue, SW, (202) 484-0206

A note from Ms. Rooney:

Also at the Tidal Basin is the Cherry Blossom Festival in March or April. The Japanese Government gave us 3,000 trees, and 4,000 more were planted. A 300-year-old Japanese lantern is lighted. A Cherry Blossom Queen is crowned.

THE MALL AND THE SMITHSONIAN INSTITUTION

Dawn Tiffany Bosco's Extra Credit Report on the Mall and the Smithsonian Institution:

In between the Capitol Building and the Lincoln Memorial is a wide grassy strip. It's called the *Mall.* Play on the grass, or sit and watch the Frisbee players. On each side are museums. The red brick building with the towers is called the *Castle.* Go into this building first. You can find out about the *Smithsonian Institution*'s thirteen museums. See which ones you want to visit.

The Mall runs between Constitution and Independence avenues. The Castle is at Tenth Street and Jefferson Drive. Hint: All the Smithsonians have the same telephone number, (202) 357-2700.

THE NATIONAL AIR AND SPACE MUSEUM

Derrick Grace says:

Emily Arrow and I say the *National Air and Space Museum* is the best. We could spend days trying to see everything. Old planes. Satellites. Spacecraft. There's the Wright Brothers' Kitty Hawk Flyer from 1903, and the X-1 aircraft, which was the first to fly faster than sound. You'll see a red plane. It was

Amelia Earhart's. She was the first woman to fly across the Atlantic Ocean. You can walk through *Skylab* and find out how the astronauts live. If you're interested in stars, don't miss the planetarium.

Independence Avenue between Fourth and Seventh streets, (202) 357-2700

THE ARTS AND INDUSTRIES BUILDING

Mr. Bell told the gym class:

The *Arts and Industries Building* is great. You'll see things that were shown at the Philadelphia Centennial Exposition. And that was in 1876. There's a locomotive engine, boat models, furniture, and a Liberty Bell made out of sugar. If you'd like to see a live show, send for Discovery Theater's program.

900 Jefferson Drive, SW, (202) 357-2700; Discovery Theater: (202) 357-1500

THE HIRSHHORN MUSEUM
AND SCULPTURE GARDEN

Mrs. Clark, third-grade teacher, told Emily Arrow:
 I really liked the *Hirshhorn Museum and Sculpture Garden*. If you can picture being inside a doughnut, you'll know what this building looks like. Huge pieces of art are hung on the larger walls, and smaller pieces on the smaller walls. You can see cartoons and hear stories on Saturdays during the school year. The sculpture garden outside is fun to see too.

Seventh Street and Independence Avenue, SW,
(202) 357-2700

The Arthur M. Sackler Gallery,
the National Museum of African Art,
and the Freer Gallery of Art

Mrs. Kara, the art teacher, writes:

You can guess I'd like the *Arthur M. Sackler Gallery*. This underground museum has Asian paintings, jewelry, and beautiful objects from as early as 4000 B.C. A monthly calendar will tell you about workshops, storytelling, and other events.

> 1050 Independence Avenue, SW, (202) 357-2700

Mrs. Kara also likes:

The *National Museum of African Art*. You'll think you've taken a trip to Africa. Don't miss the statues and masks.

> 950 Independence Avenue, SW, (202) 357-2700

And she likes:

The *Freer Gallery of Art*. This is a huge group of American and Asian art. You'll see Chinese jade, Indian miniatures, and the beautiful Peacock Room.

Twelfth Street and Jefferson Drive, SW, (202) 357-2700

THE NATIONAL MUSEUM OF AMERICAN HISTORY

Mrs. Miller, the Killer, the substitute teacher, says:

I hope you'll visit the *National Museum of American History*. This is a wonderful house of treasures. You'll see the flag that Francis Scott Key saw when he wrote "The Star-Spangled Banner." Some of the toys used by children who lived in the White House are here, and gowns worn by the presidents' wives. You'll even spot the ruby slippers from *The Wizard of Oz*.

Fourteenth Street between Constitution Avenue and Madison Drive, (202) 357-2700

THE NATIONAL MUSEUM OF NATURAL HISTORY

Class Project:

We studied The *National Museum of Natural History*. It has the Hope Diamond. That's the largest diamond in the world. It has lots of other stuff too. At the Naturalist Center is a huge dinosaur, a triceratops. Everyone calls him Uncle Beazley. Some of the other huge things are a blue whale and an African elephant. They're not alive, but you can see the live insects at the insect zoo. A skillion bees are flying around in their hives, and there are ant-hills. It makes us itchy to think about it . . . but we loved it.

Tenth Street and Constitution Avenue, NW, (202) 357-2700

THE SMITHSONIAN CAROUSEL

Matthew Jackson writes:

Take a three-minute ride on the *Smithsonian Carousel*. Don't get dizzy dizzy dizzy dizzy dizzy dizzy dizzy dizzy dizzy dizzy dizzy dizzy dizzy dizzy dizzy . . .

On the Mall, near the Smithsonian Castle, Tenth Street and Constitution Avenue, SW

Jill Simon's father says:

I love the *National Zoological Park,* the Zoo. Almost any animal, snake, or bird you'd want to see is here. Hsing-Hsing is a giant panda, given to the children of America by China. You can watch him being fed . . . as well as lions, tigers, and other animals. Don't miss the Herplab for movies and puzzles and the chance to see a snake up close.

3001 Connecticut Avenue, NW, (202) 357-2700

The Pierce Mill

Jill Simon's mother says:

In 1820, Isaac Pierce built a barn, a springhouse, and a mill that are still there. Visit the *Pierce Mill* and watch them grind corn and wheat. Watch the falling water at the waterwheel.

Rock Creek Park at Beach Drive and Tilden Street, NW, (203) 426-6908

The Bureau of Engraving and Printing

Timothy Barbiero says:

I like the *Bureau of Engraving and Printing* best. Did you know a dollar bill doesn't last even two years? I guess that's why they're always printing new ones. You can see them being made right here. You can see stamps being printed too. You can even buy a bag of shredded money.

Wallenburg Place, Fifteenth and C streets, SW, (202) 622-2000

Mrs. Kara says:

I have to tell you another super place: *The National Gallery of Art*. There are two buildings, the East and the West. Outside the East Building is a sculpture you can hide in. Inside are many colorful pieces of modern art. Andy Warhol's soup cans, for example. For earlier art, cross over to the West Building. Use the tunnel to see the glassed-in waterfall.

Fourth Street at Constitution Avenue, (202) 737-4215

The National Archives

A note from Ms. Rooney:

At the *National Archives*, you can see two pages of the Declaration of Independence, the Bill of Rights, and the Constitution. These papers from the beginnings of our country are very special. Every night they're put in a fireproof space deep under the floor.

> Constitution Avenue between Seventh and Ninth streets, NW, (202) 501-5000

The United States Botanic Gardens

Jim the custodian wants you to know . . .

If you like plants, go to the *United States Botanic Gardens*. It's a huge greenhouse with over 10,000 types of plants. I like the orchids, the pineapple and tapioca plants, and the chocolate trees!

> Maryland Avenue near First Street, SW, (202) 255-8333

THE PHILLIPS COLLECTION

A Special Report by Linda Lorca and Sherri Dent:
   The *Phillips Collection* is the oldest permanent museum of modern art in the United States. It has the work of some of the world's most famous artists. It has a children's program too. Write for information on parent-child workshops.

> 1600 Twenty-first Street, NW, (202) 387-0961

THE FREDERICK DOUGLASS
NATIONAL HISTORIC SITE

Extra Credit by Wayne O'Brien and Alex Walker:
   Go to the *Frederick Douglass National Historic Site.* Frederick Douglass was the son of a slave. He fought hard for everyone to have equal rights. This is the house where he lived. There's a film about his life. You can take a tour of the rooms.

> 1411 W Street, SE, (202) 426-5960

THE JOHN F. KENNEDY CENTER
FOR THE PERFORMING ARTS

A last note from Ms. Rooney:

The John F. Kennedy Center for the Performing Arts is a wonderful place to visit. There are flags from every state . . . and from almost every country in the world. You can see plays or music programs for children at the Theater for Young People.

New Hampshire Avenue at Rock Creek Parkway, NW, (202) 467-4600

About the Author/About the Artist

Patricia Reilly Giff is the author of more than fifty books for young readers, including the Kids of the Polk Street School books, the Lincoln Lions Marching Band books, and the Polka Dot Private Eye books. She lives in Weston, Connecticut.

Blanche Sims has illustrated all of the Polk Street books. She lives in Westport, Connecticut.